By Wright Morris

*Novels*
A Life (1973)
War Games (1972)
Fire Sermon (1971)
In Orbit (1967)
One Day (1965)
Cause For Wonder (1963)
What A Way To Go (1962)
Ceremony In Lone Tree (1960)
Love Among The Cannibals (1957)
The Field Of Vision (1956)
The Huge Season (1954)
The Deep Sleep (1953)
The Works Of Love (1952)
Man And Boy (1951)
The World In The Attic (1949)
The Man Who Was There (1945)
My Uncle Dudley (1942)

*Stories*
Green Grass, Blue Sky, White House (1970)

*Photo-Text*
Love Affair: A Venetian Journal (1972)
God's Country And My People (1968)
The Home Place (1948)
The Inhabitants (1946)

*Essays*
A Bill Of Rites, A Bill Of Wrongs, A Bill Of Goods (1968)
The Territory Ahead (1958)

*Anthology*
Wright Morris: A Reader (1970)

# HERE IS WRIGHT
# EINBAUM MORRIS

*Los Angeles*
BLACK SPARROW PRESS
*1973*

"Here Is Einbaum" and "A Fight Between a White Boy and a Black Boy in the Dusk of a Fall Afternoon in Omaha, Nebraska" originally appeared in *The New Yorker;* "Magic" in *The Southern Review;* "Fiona" in *Esquire;* and "In Another Country" in *The Atlantic Monthly.*

LIBRARY OF CONGRESS CATALOGING IN PUBLICATION DATA

Morris, Wright, 1910-
  Here is Einbaum.

    CONTENTS: Here is Einbaum—Magic.—A fight between a white boy and a black boy in the dusk of a fall afternoon in Omaha, Nebraska. [etc.]
    I.  Title.
PZ3.M8346He  [PS3525.07475]    813'.5'2    73-11149
 ISBN 0-87685-164-2
 ISBN 0-87685-163-4 (pbk.)
 ISBN 0-87685-165-0 (lim. ed.)

# CONTENTS

Here Is Einbaum .......................... 9

Magic ................................. .. 29

A Fight Between a White Boy and
  a Black Boy in the Dusk of a Fall
  Afternoon in Omaha, Nebraska ............. 49

Fiona ...................................... 57

In Another Country ........................ 71

HERE IS EINBAUM

Here is Einbaum at an open casement window, three floors above the street. On the corner just below him, barefooted, a beggar stands in the fresh fall of snow. His head is bare. He has tipped his face so that Einbaum can see his beard. Before him, in an attitude of prayer, the palms of his hands are pressed together, with a narrow slit for coins between his thumbs. He sings. Someone from a window below Einbaum has tossed him a coin. It is searched for in the snow by two shabby children and the woman who holds a third child at her hip. The head and feet of this child are bare, but it looks well fed. Einbaum has been told that these cunning beggars rent the children from people who have too many, but the woman who told him this is the one who dropped the coin. What is he to believe—that she is wrong, or merely a fool? Until he was told, he sometimes dropped a coin himself. When the beggar sang Christmas carols, the children joined in, their mouths round and dark in their pale white faces. Einbaum's delight was in the sensation that they were needy and he could help them; his torment in the certain knowledge that he was a fool. In the room behind Einbaum the ceiling is high and his sister, Ilse, sits sewing on buttons. She is paid by the button. Her scalp gleams white at the part of her hair. Einbaum steps back from the window to let the housemaid, Karina, air out the bolster and puff the pillows, and they both stand waiting, knowing that the dust will make her sneeze.

Here is Einbaum in the woods of the Wienerwald, concealed by

9

shadows and leaves. He lies sprawled on his face; we see only the soles of his boots and the rucksack strapped to his back. One arm is crooked beneath his head. The other grips an unloaded miltary rifle. Einbaum is in the midst of the training exercises he enjoys much more than he does his freedom. He is good at it. He can tramp with his pack eighteen miles a day. In his group it is openly admitted that if there is war Einbaum will rise fast. He likes to serve. He likes the simple orderly life. On him and around him glows the golden light of a melancholy Viennese fall, the leaves crushed by lovers who have been careful to stub their cigarettes.

Here is Einbaum at the Studenten Klub, seated at the window overlooking the Schottengasse: snow is falling. It blurs the Christmas lights and the spire of Stefansdom. Einbaum strains to read the time on the glowing face of a clock. The woman seated at his side is his mistress, Frau Koenig. She wears galoshes that are wet and give off an odor. He is only at his ease with her, she tells him, when they are in bed. Little if anything ever said to Einbaum, up to this moment, has pleased him so much. Einbaum the heartless rogue. Einbaum the callous sensualist. It is unimportant, for the time being, that he is also not at ease with her in bed. Part of the problem is technical. He sometimes fears he might suffocate. Her gloved hands rest on her wide matron's lap. Frau Koenig hasn't given him much pleasure, but she has given Einbaum great plans. He will be a roué. Generous matrons will support him in the manner to which he will one day be accustomed. As the snow falls he wonders what time it is. Frau Koenig will misinterpret Einbaum's glancing at his watch, which happened to be the one she gave him. Now it is Christmas. Before buying her something he would like to know what she intends to give him.

We might doubt it, but this, too, is Einbaum. He wears a bowler and carries a valise. It is heavy with books necessary to his life at the University. Two volumes of Spengler, Count Keyserling's

10

"Travel Diary," one book of Italian grammar, another of Italian history. There is also a separate folder of notes, written in code. Einbaum the revolutionary, the *agent provocateur*, waits on the steps of the University for a colleague from Graz, Herr L— (Einbaum will always see it with the letters missing), who, with Einbaum, will create the disturbance initiating the new order in Vienna. The password is *"Oesterreich über alles,"* unlikely as it seems. While running from this scene, which proved to be a fiasco, he is pursued by a man no larger than Dollfuss, who fires a shot that turns up in the second volume of Einbaum's Spengler— a lead pellet he later attached to the fob of his watch. He liked intrigue. He considered an offer that would set him up, comfortably, in Buda. It was one of his options when something more interesting intervened.

Once more, here is Einbaum—but does it matter? Everyone has an album full of such snapshots. Few, of course, were ever taken by the camera, but they remain indelible on the lens of the eye. In the dark, as a rule, one sees them the clearest, glowing like figures of the face of a watch. Why these and not others? Einbaum often wonders. Something to do with his own life and torment. He cannot spell it out, but in these recurring snapshots the film of his life had its reruns. He studied it for clues to what later happened: some inkling, some suggestion, of emerging powers. Nothing unusual. The same vague apprehensions common to millions of German Jews. Mendelssohn Einbaum often feared for his life, but that was hardly news.

With shame he admits it, but a German first. Both sides of the family burghers in Linz, where they specialized in leather tanning. Einbaum's Jewish grandfather used to say Austria is a condition from which Germans must recover. Perhaps Einbaum did not. He was born in Vienna—his mother, Elsa Nottebaum, an actress of some importance in Hofmannsthal's plays. Einbaum's

11

grandmother wore the family jewels on a cord between her breasts, where they acquired a patina. Is it possible to be a German and a Jew? Einbaum stands before you. Other people's clothes fit him better than his own. The way he backs into a chair, or crooks his finger into the coin slot of a pay phone, the way he nods his head, like a finger, when speaking, or juts it forward, wagging, when listening, the way his coat gapes open like a tent flap—but the impression is clearer across the room than when face to face. A German, unmistakably, and more or less mistakably, a Jew. Was it the German or the Jew in him that seemed to be the clearest that day in August, 1939? The century was ten years older than Einbaum. He walked in a drizzle on Kärntnerstrasse. Where the street bends and opens on Stefansdom he stepped from the curb to make way for two ladies. The hair of one was damp. His face actually brushed it as he dipped his head beneath her umbrella. It is why a moment passes before he notes the cab pulled up beside him at the curb. From the lowered rear window a gloved hand beckons. Einbaum peers around. At the moment he stands alone, so it must be him. "Frau Koenig?" he says, sure that it must be, and he is half into the cab before he knows better. It is a fine scene: Einbaum bodily abducted in the full light of day. This woman in the cab he knows casually from the musical evenings at the Studenten Klub, and from pictures of her in the *Wiener Tagblatt* skiing in the Alps or playing tennis. A peasant, physically, she has wrists and ankles that are thicker and stronger than Einbaum's. Her blue eyes are much too small for her broad, blond face. Not that it mattered; small or not, they had singled out and selected Einbaum. More important to the scene, as time would prove, was the scent, both animal and mineral, into which Einbaum dipped his head. The day was humid. In such weather everything smells. It left the cab with her, however, and Einbaum would come to know it as the *fleur de peur*, the scent of fear that she never lost. Soon enough, alas, everything else would be taken from the Countess Horvath-Szapati but this odor—and Mendelssohn Einbaum. Neither was ever lost.

Was it with this incident that everything of interest might be said to have begun? The summer of 1939, the city of Vienna was like a shabby unaired museum full of aging attendants and apprehensive tourists, where young men and women of Einbaum's age lived with dreams already buried. Vienna was not music to Einbaum, nor the sight of the bedding of lovers at the casement windows, nor *Kaffee mit Schlag,* nor a dying way of life, nor any of the many things he discussed with his friends or read in the *Neue Wiener Zeitung.* In those days he carried a card engraved with the name of Mendelssohn Einbaum. He used the tip of his cane to flip leaves from the sidewalk and, with the Countess, a Hungarian from Pest, attended the séances of Lady Golding-Brieslau in her apartment on Schottengasse. Einbaum liked the atmosphere of anxiety, dread, and childish awe. At the ringing of bells his heart pounded. The odor of fear was stronger than the incense. Regardless of what happened, Einbaum himself felt cleansed and one of the chosen to have survived it. He felt he understood the appeal of the Mass without the nonsense of the faith. Besides elderly women, he also met people of unusual background or superior attainments.

Countess Horvath-Szapati played remarkable tennis and had a scholarly interest, like her father, in church history. She spoke, in addition to German and Hungarian, excellent English and French. With a deliberation that was characteristic she used Einbaum to practice her French, skillfully fending off his efforts to practice his English. She talked of going to Brazil. Her father, Count Horvath, had mining interests that would profit from her personal supervison. She had the cunning and assurance of a Cossack. Frizzly straw-colored hair topped her large, round skull,

13

seamlessly joined to her shoulders. Indoors she perspired. In the dimmed light of the séance her face gleamed like gold leaf. All the features were too small, more like those of a child than a woman, the small pointed teeth busily nibbling at her wind-chapped lips. Hardly a beauty or a charmer, the Countess Horvath-Szapati had a somewhat puzzling but magnetic attraction. Her eyes sparkled. Something to do with animal vitality. Einbaum was not alone in the thought he had given to how a man might seduce such a woman, if that was the word. Her thighs were enormous. In her frequent rages at tennis blunders she would snap the racquet in her hands like pastry. What did she want with French? She considered it the language of confidences. Einbaum's inside track, insofar as he had one, lay in his superior knowledge of the French subjunctive. The question of what to *do* with money, for instance, or jewels, seemed amusing and plausible when discussed in French. It was possible to be remarkably intimate, and yet impersonal. French novels were specific, if not up-to-date. There were also imaginary problems of travel, decisions about luggage, and questions of climate. Heat she did not like. Her favorite high place in Europe seemed to be in Gavarnie, in the Pyrenees. One could see it on a poster in the lobby of the American Express. She liked high places. She liked the white silence of a world of snow. Einbaum, in contrast, felt himself especially drawn to lower altitudes and more open space. The American Wild West appealed to Einbaum—what he had seen of it in the movies. Man and nature harmoniously blended. The savage beauty and simplicity of the Indian. In the Historical Museum, Einbaum had paused to examine the feathered headgear of the chiefs, and their bows and arrows. Remote as cavemen, yet alive at the time Einbaum's Grandfather Nottebaum came from Prague to Vienna, the Battle of Balaklava the high point of his long life.

Einbaum loved the movies and felt they were related, in a way,

14

to the séance. One sat in the dark and waited for materializations; at the movies they occurred. To Einbaum's taste, these appearances were more gratifying than the ringing of bells, the table knockings, and the voices that the Countess found so impressive. Although a devout Catholic, she liked the reassurance of a more physical survival. The spiritual she took for granted. No doctrine justified a belief in the spirit's return to the flesh, but she felt there might be progress in this area. The purpose of religion, quite simply, was to dispense with the problem of death. A start had been made, but fulfillment would come when the spirit recovered the flesh it had lost. Einbaum saw it as part of her primitive, Magyar inheritance. It amused him that this indestructible woman seemed so concerned with her life elsewhere. She wore a jeweled cross, a scarab ring, and carried in her purse cabalistic objects to increase her luck and frighten away evil spirits. To what end? Yet Einbaum noted he felt safer in her company.

As the summer waned, Einbaum helped the Countess shop for what she might need in her travels. It was not clear where; that would be the last decision she would make. He rode about with her in taxis, holding her purchases. In the confines of the cab, if not concealed by the smell of her rubbers, or of her wet coat and umbrella, Einbaum was aware, as in a shuttered sickroom, of the odor of the patient, or the illness. This woman who smelled of money, health, and assurance also gave off the sweet-sour scent of fear. An essence—like that in stoppered bottles—puffed out of her clothes when she sagged into a chair. Was it death she feared? Was she ill with more than apprehension? The straw-yellow hair, the ice-blue eyes, the face as broad and flat as a trowel concealed from others, but not from her, the dram of tainted blood that troubled her thoughts. In diplomatic French she admitted to Einbaum that they had more in common than met the eye. In her father's blood Sophia Kienholz, a Jewess, had left the strain that his daughter, among others, thought apparent. Not anything in particular—no, nothing like that. One simply sensed it was there, as one sensed it in Einbaum. The Jewishness. The *je ne sais quoi*, as the French would say. Einbaum was quick to appreciate the confidence, and share their mutual bond and apprehension. So much for the secretly tainted Count Horvath. But what did this have to do with the openly tainted Einbaum?

They were in the *Kaffeehaus* frequented by musicians, on the Lindengasse. Einbaum had taken his coffee *mit Schlag,* and sat dunking the puff with his spoon. Conspiracies he liked. In French they ran smoother and promised more reward. In public the Countess frequently wore gloves to conceal the rings embedded in her fingers, but the kid leather fit so snugly it bore a clear imprint of the stones. There had been no discussion about how to conceal the jewels she could not take off. Einbaum was inexperienced, but not indifferent to the nuances and complexities of his emotions. He liked the drama. He vaguely sensed that the drama, with the passage of time, would prove to be of more interest than the crisis. With one gloved finger the Countess Horvath-Szapati pressed her lip to where her teeth could nibble a raw spot, her eyes flickering from side to side to show the charge of her thought. Einbaum was thinking somebody should paint her, regretting that he lacked the talent. This cunning blond peasant disguised as a countess had reason for her apprehension. What reason did she have for Einbaum?

In the opinion of the Countess, Mendelssohn Einbaum bore a remarkable resemblance to Count Horvath. The same stocky frame, with no neck to speak of. The deferent, attentive manner of a good headwaiter. Also a good listener, with an almost inaudible voice. The Count was a student of Ottoman history and spent most of his time living privately, among his books, or hunting in the forests of Abony, the family estate neighboring Pest. He saw

16

few people; outside of family friends, even fewer saw him. If Einbaum, for instance, occupied the Count's quarters—with the knowledge of a few close servants—and went through his usual habits, or stayed in his quarters, he (the Count) might not actually be missed for weeks, possibly months. That would prove to be more than enough time for the Countess and her father, traveling different routes to the same destination, to be in Brazil, Guatemala, Gavarnie, in the Pyrenees, or possibly the Canary Islands, before his absence was noted. Einbaum, in the meantime, would have broken no law and his impersonation would have been purely accidental. As a friend of the Countess, he had been a guest on the estate. He could stay on, or he could return to Vienna as soon as he had received word from the Countess. Einbaum, of course, would do this as a favor, but the Countess would see to it that he was rewarded. One of the rings from her fingers would make it worth his trouble, if that was what it would take.

Had Einbaum forgotten that he, too, was a Jew? Perhaps he had never felt it so strongly. Besides, he was no Horvath and had nothing to lose but his life. In August of 1939, in Vienna, it was hard to imagine who would take Einbaum's. There were laws on the statute books. High in the council of the city of Linz was an influential uncle, husband of an Einbaum. Besides, the minor risks involved appealed to him. Not for nothing had Einbaum been a student of the gangster film and the Wild West.

Einbaum himself made the boat reservations for their trip to Budapest, on the seventh of September. That was the season for river outings, and they were certain to be seen by innumerable people. For this excursion Einbaum bought himself a trenchcoat, of the sort popular with Germans, and a cane often seen at the races, with the handles forming a saddle the observer could sit on. That was not all. The metal shaft contained a glass tube for several ounces of brandy or kirschwasser. When it was not in use, he

17

wore it in the crook of his arm.

Thus matters stood on the first day of September, the day Hitler invaded Poland. Just one day later, with a servant named Rudi, who carried several pairs of skis along with other luggage, the Countess and Einbaum took a train for a ski resort in the Italian Alps. They left the train at Graz, however, and went by car to a village on the Hungarian border. Count Horvath, perhaps without luggage, would arrive on the bus that left Pest that morning. He would take Einbaum's seat on the train; Einbaum would return to Pest on the bus. If there were complications, the Countess would return to Pest and they would make new plans. The bus from Pest appeared on schedule, before midnight, but Count Horvath was not on it. A briefcase with his initials, containing a bottle of akvavit, two Swiss chocolate bars, and a phial of sleeping powders, was found on one of the seats. Without a word Sophia Szapati took one of her ski poles and beat the driver of the bus as she would a horse. When Einbaum tried to restrain her, she beat him. The metal tip left the scar still visible through his beard. All of this was observed by the servant Rudi, from his seat on the pile of luggage. He waited both for help and for the seizure to pass. This side of her temperament was new to Einbaum, and so was her grief. Was it her affection for the Count, or merely the interruption of her plans? Nothing would console her. She bolted the door to her room in the inn, but her shoes were there in the morning for Rudi to polish. First things first. Later that day, inanely gay, as if drugged, her mouth frozen in the smile of an animal trainer, she appeared at Einbaum's door to tell him that marriage would simplify their travel problems. Had she lost her mind? The point seemed academic. She still had more mind to lose than Einbaum. Nothing at Einbaum's disposal had the power to deflect her will. There would be delays, thanks

18

to complications, and Einbaum thought he read the script as a staged performance, an act of hysteria that met her needs but for which she might not be responsible later. Shock, they called it. Einbaum would come to know much about shock.

In practical terms, the novels of intrigue supplied them both with a pattern of action. Little seemed new. All of this had been done so often before. Stranger couples than Einbaum and the Countess were seen on trains out of Vienna, and their story would not surprise the porter she had generously tipped. The servant Rudi had been blessed, put on the bus, and sent back to Pest. Strange that Einbaum, rocking in a berth euphoric with akvavit and the rising elevation, should remark that he had seldom felt so good about the future at the moment the lights were going out over Europe. How explain it? He was by nature a gentle, even apprehensive, man.

Money got them to Spain. The plane itself, a kite with open cockpits, recruited in Gorizia, was worth less than the money they paid for the passage, but she enjoyed the flight. At a moment her fear, accumulating for hours, would release itself in exhilaration —the thrill of a child rocking the seat of a Ferris wheel. Einbaum was terrified. He sat so long with stiff, clasped hands he had no feeling in his fingers. Wind filled his ears at night. They might have flown on to Lisbon, and from there to New York, but the travel agent could find few listings and accommodations under "Skiing." Before they flew on to Brazil, where little snow fell, the Countess wanted a last winter of skiing, and a chance to reconsider her plans for the future. The war might soon be over. Privately, she feared the godless Russians more than the Germans.

With her two sets of skis and shoe skates for Einbaum—along with wool mittens and matching fur earmuffs—they went north to a village in the Spanish Pyrenees that proved to be jammed with refugee traffic. There was little skiing. There was also a shortage of rooms and beds. The rumor was that ports of exit, in either direction, were in the hands of spies or Nazi sympathizers, and all foreigners, particularly Jews, were subject to investigation, their possessions confiscated. Was it possible? Einbaum thought it possible.

Countess Horvath-Szapati, travelling alone, with the added inducement of a little jewelry, might fly off to do her skiing elsewhere. Then again she might not. Although she was fond, as she said, of Einbaum, and talked to him as she would to a priest, her feelings, as well as her affections, followed the custom of a master and a servant. Frankly, Einbaum rather liked it. It testified to her breeding, as her appearance did not. On the vantage side, for Einbaum, this proved to mean that she needed him more than he needed her. She was accustomed to a Rudi, or a Helga, or a pet—she was subject to weeping for a hound, Süsschen, that slept on her bed and licked her awake—to be there at her side, at her service, or within range of her voice. The division of the men and women made necessary by the crowding—into separate groups, occupying separate dormitories—was a greater hardship on the Countess than the incident at the border. She could not stand the lack of privacy; she could not stand absolute privacy. Without Einbaum she lost her wits. She made a fool of herself among the women, pointing out that she, Sophia Szapati, was a countess, and offering to make it worth the while of those with the taste to recognize it. Women with that sort of taste were not lacking. The Countess's ingroup, a half-dozen or more females he was never given the opportunity to study, occupied a corner of the dormitory screened off from the room with several bedsheets. Among them was a Spanish Jewess, a lean bitter woman Einbaum thought he might have seen later in the movie "La Strada"—one of the faces uplifted to the performer on the high wire. A cardinal principle of the Countess was that Jews could be bought. She let it be known that she would buy her way out, preferably through France, when the winter was over. She liked the language. She would take up residence in Paris. This should have upset Einbaum or made him apprehensive, but his temperament displayed a chronic weakness: people amazed him. What would they think of next? His anger at human folly was not equal to the pleasure observing it gave him. This remarkable woman, known to him as a countess, could change her spots when the *script* called for it. The word "script" was Einbaum's. It seemed appropriate to the cast and the circumstances. Here in the Pyrenees, as in an ambitious movie, several thousand strangers were locked in a drama of waiting. Einbaum did not merely endure it. No, as the tension mounted, he speculated on its resolution. Along with hunches and calculated guesses, there was increasingly the question of people. Like francs, pesetas, and dollars, they were negotiable. Some would prove to cash in, others to check out. As an example, the Countess, for all her discomfort, was at her best when she *hated* something. That she had in abundance. It brought out in her a vitality, a passion, that Einbaum associated with more intimate matters. This cow of a woman aroused desire. Einbaum marked it in himself. She slept in the clothes she feared she might lose, with her valuables worn on a chain at her armpit. Einbaum had seen them, green as American money, when she raised her arms to put up her hair. Someone had told her this patina would increase their value, testifying to their age. Cash money she kept in a fold of flesh at her waist.

One morning at sunrise, the village still in the shadow of the snowcapped peaks to the east, Einbaum was awakened by a boy, Alexis, and hurriedly taken to the women's quarters. Most of them slept. There had been no disturbance to wake them up. The stale air had the sickening sweetness Einbaum associated with the

21

female period. In the favored location, for which she had paid, set off from the cots of her ingroup, Sophia Szapati sprawled on her back as if stoned. A wet towel had been placed on her forehead and eyes, but her mouth stood open. In such a bulk, how small it looked. A quilt pressed between her flanks, where someone had kneeled. Among other things too numerous to mention, the Countess Szapati had lost the gold crowns to her teeth. Someone had propped open the jaws, fished them out. Einbaum had the impression of a crudely looted piece of antique statuary, known to have had rare gems for eyes and solid gold teeth. Nevertheless, the over-all impression was comical. A beached and looted hulk, or ship's prow, waiting for the tide to sweep it out to sea. The ring promised to Einbaum had been cunningly cut from her finger. On her spacious behind—she had been rolled on her face by an official who knew what to look for, and where—a spot no larger than a pinprick indicated the point where the needle had entered. Perhaps it had never left. (Einbaum had heard the stories of how they circulated like fish in the bloodstream.) This grotesque incident would not have occurred in the orderly rigor of a well-run police state, and owed its success to the relaxed confusion of the time and place. Friends and enemies were not clearly defined— a situation she instinctively feared. The consensus was that she had been the victim of the impression she left on others. Nothing would kill her. So she had had the benefit of too great a dose. The frail and cunning were better qualified to survive.

Einbaum's health actually improved on the camp rations and absence of tobacco. The letters Einbaum might have written for himself he wrote for others in French, German, and English. Few were answered. Einbaum was not tempted to try his luck. The past so desperately cherished by others held little attraction for him. Nor did the flight to Brazil, Canada, or the United States. Confinement gratified something in his temperament. An elderly

22

Jew, Klugmann, who asked Einbaum's help with his Double-Crostics, diagnosed Einbaum's contentment as a return to the womb of the ghetto. Here in the camp he was at home. In a condition of freedom was he ill at ease? Klugmann had practiced psychoanalysis in Prague, where the anxiety of the Jews, if they had not been dispersed by war and incineration, would have tested Klugmann's theory that fear was more productive of spiritual renewal than hope. Now it hung in the air. Klugmann talked in this way while Einbaum dozed over the gaps in Klugmann's Double-Crostics—an American entertainment supplied to him by the secretary of the American Friends Service Committee, a society of Quakers. The Crostics came to her from a friend in New York by the name of Bettina Gernsprecher. It was Einbaum who took the trouble to write and thank her for them both.

Here is Einbaum in New York. A greeting-card salesman, he has the use of one of the company's imported Volvos. The president is a Swede, a strong believer in foreign trade. Einbaum's area is in Bucks County, where his knowledge of German is considered an advantage. His manner is friendly, but his speech is sort of muttering, and the talk slacks off. There is something annoying about Einbaum, but it goes unmentioned, being hard to define. What is appealing is obvious. Einbaum is human. He has lived, like you, an already long and pointless life. He is on the road four or five days a week, and looks forward to sleeping late on Sundays. While in the city Einbaum stays with Bettina Gernsprecher, who colors the greeting cards by hand. The outline is there, and Bettina is free to vary the colors of the lips, the hair, and the eyes. This costs the buyer extra, but it gives Bettina a steady job. It takes eight months of the year to prepare for the seasonal rushes. Bettina sits on a stool, her back arched over so the bones protrude like knuckles, her knees drawn up to support the clipboard and the card. She puts a point to the brush by twisting it on her lips. Einbaum has warned her. He has told her the story of the women who died from painting numerals on watch faces—those that glow in the dark. Bettina's cards do not glow as yet, but one day they might. On his trips to the city Einbaum brings her his laundry, and while they listen to music she darns his socks. She likes to darn. She cannot sit for long without using her hands.

Early pictures of Bettina are lacking, since they were destroyed with the ghetto in Cracow. Because she was tall for her age, a place was made for her in a brothel limited to Jewish females. This information she shared with Einbaum the Sunday they went to the Met together. Humiliation, remorse, even self-disgust are sentiments that she has dispensed with. There is skill in her hands. She received her training in a concentration camp. She paid her own way when Einbaum took her to lunch, and shared with him the lower half of her daybed. Stretched at his side, or beneath him, she was taller, but her chronic stoop brought her eye to eye with him in elevators. Einbaum saw very little of her when they walked in the street. He found himself, soon enough, either a stride or two behind her or several strides ahead and pausing to wait for her. During her formative years, she had either been led (she found it hard to remember) or pushed from behind.

It is not easily explained that a woman's age and appearance seem irrelevant. Einbaum talked a good deal; could it be said she listened? When Einbaum showered, he would find looped over the curtain rail her brassiere with the padded cups: if a woman really cared *that* much, why didn't she care more? Another time he found a shirt that was not his own in the laundry he brought back from the city. A small neck size, but the arms of an ape. Einbaum returned the shirt without comment, and that was where the matter rested.

Nevertheless, in her company he was subject to puzzling sensations. Years after any woman had been seen with a bob, Bettina found it a sensible hair style. The hair in front she cut herself, and let the barber apply clippers at the back. Einbaum could not make up his mind if he thought her a new and higher form of life or a lower. Her detachment extended beyond the things of this world. It was the contrary—he felt obliged to point out—with Sophia Szapati, the other woman in his life. She had been attached to things until death and thieves took them from her. "Looted" was the word. Einbaum had frequently described the spectacle for Bettina. The puzzling thing was that these two women, for all their differences, had one thing in common. They had chosen Einbaum. It could not be said that he had actually chosen them. Sophia had all but kidnapped him in Vienna, beckoning to him from the back seat of the taxi, and Bettina Gernsprecher, sight unseen, had agreed to support him until he found work, persuading her employer with the ape-long arms to hire Einbaum as a greeting-card salesman.

So here is Einbaum—through, as we say, no fault of his own.

MAGIC

Robert could see Father in the front seat, steering. He could see Mother and the lover in the back seat, sitting. They came around the lake past the Japanese lanterns and Mrs. Van Zant's idea of a birthday party. The car stopped and Father got out and opened the door for Mother. Mother got out and pulled her dress down. She leaned back in and said, "Here we are—here we are, lover!"

"I object to your sentimentality," said Father.

"Here we are, lover," Mother said, and pulled him out of the car. His arms stuck out of the sleeves of his coat. One pocket of his pants was pulled inside out. Robert wanted to see the bump on his head but he had on his hat. "Here we are," Mother said, and turned him to look at Robert.

"This is Mr. Brady, son," said Father.

"I told you," Mother said, "Callie's boyfriend."

"Where's Callie?" said Robert.

"Callie's got her lungs full of water, baby. She's where they'll dry her out."

"He's dried out?" asked Robert. He didn't look it. There was a line around his hat where the water had stopped. Under the hat, where he had the bump, Mother said his head was shaved. "Why'd she hit him?"

"She didn't hit him, baby. He fell on it. When they fell out of the boat he fell on it."

"A likely story," Father said. "Is that Emily?"

29

Robert's sister Emily stood in the door holding one of Robert's rabbits and wearing both of Callie's slippers.

"Go put your clothes on!" Father said.

"My God, why?" cried Mother. "She's cute as cotton. Why would anybody put some lousy clothes on it?"

"Don't shout!" shouted Father.

To the lover Emily said, "Did you ever hug a rabbit?"

"He doesn't want to hug a rabbit," Father said, "or see little girls with all their clothes off."

"Why not?" Mother said.

"Mr. Brady is not well," said Father. "When he fell from the boat he bumped his head and was injured."

"Where does he hurt?" said Robert.

"In his heart, baby."

"Mr. Brady has lost his memory," said Father.

"What a wonderful way to be," said Mother.

"How does he do it?" asked Robert.

Father said, "You don't *do* it. It just happens. You forget to feed your rabbits. He has forgotten his name."

"Isn't he wonderful?" Mother said. She took his hand. "You must be starving!"

"They said he had just eaten," said Father. "Where you going to put him?"

"Did Callie lose her memory too?" asked Robert.

Mother said, "No such luck, baby—"

"She has some water in her lungs," said Father, "but she didn't lose her memory. She said she wanted you in bed."

To Emily, Mother said, "Is that the *same* rabbit? My God, if I'm not sick of rabbits."

"Can't they dress themselves without her?" Father said. "Put down that rabbit, will you? Go put some clothes on."

"Isn't she cute as cotton?" Mother said to Mr. Brady. Emily put down the rabbit and showed her funny belly button. Robert's button went in, but Emily's button went out.

"Are you going to speak to her about that?" said Father.

"Show lover your sleeping doll, pet," said Mother.

Emily rolled her eyes back so only the whites showed. Robert called it playing dead.

"I'll show him up," Father said. "Where you putting him?"

"Callie's room!" they both cried.

To Mr. Brady, Mother said, "You like a nap? You take a nap. You take a nice nap, then we have dinner."

Father whinnied. "If Callie's not here, who's going to prepare it?"

Mother hadn't thought about it. She stood thinking, fingering the pins in her golden hair.

"We could eat pizzas!" cried Robert. "Pisa's Pizzas!"

Emily clapped her hands.

"You don't seem to grasp the situation," said Father. "You have a man on your hands. You have a legal situation."

"I hope so," said Mother.

"It's your picnic—" began Father.

"Picnic! Picnic!" Emily cried.

Father rubbed his palms together. "I'll show him up. You dress the children. You like to use the washroom, Mr. Brady?" Father led him down the hall.

Their mother took off the green hat and felt for the pins in her golden hair. She took them out like clothespins, held them in her mouth, while she raised her arms and let the fan cool beneath them. Through the open French doors she could see across the lake to Mrs. Van Zant's lawn and all the Japanese lanterns. Mrs. Van Zant lay in the hammock on the porch with her beach hat on her face. Mother gave Emily her hairpins, then threw back her

head so the hair hung down like Lady Godiva's. When she shook
her head more hairpins dropped on the polar bear rug. These pins
were for Robert. He picked them up and made a tight fistful of
them.

"What was I going to say, pet?" Mother said.

"Where's Callie," said Emily.

"In the hospital, baby. She's in Mr. Brady's head. That's why
it hurts him."

"He's got no memory?" said Robert.

"Who needs it, baby. Give Mother her pins." His mother sat
on the stool between the three mirrors with her long golden hair
parted in the middle, fanned out on her front. "Your mother is
Lady Godiva," she said.

"Lady Godiva my lawnmower!" said Father. He came through
the French doors with a drink and took a seat on the bed.

"You like horses, baby?" Mother said to Robert. "She was the
one on the horse."

"Can you picture your mother on a horse?" said Father. Ho-ho-
ho, he laughed.

"Tell your father he's no lover," said Mother.

"Tell your mother you could all have done worse," said Father.
"Her looks, my brains."

"I'm not sure he understands her," said Mother. "You think
he thinks she meant to hit him?"

Father said, "Just so she didn't lose any more than he did."

"She won't like it," said Mother. "She likes to make her own
bed and eat her own food. Did you see it? White fish, white
sauce, white potatoes, white napkins. I thought I'd puke."

"In my opinion," said Father, "he jumped out of that boat. He
tried to drown himself."

"That's love for you," Mother said. "Your father wouldn't
understand."

32

"It's a miracle he *didn't* drown," said Father.

"See how your father sits and stares," said Mother.

"Ppp-shawww, I'm too old for that stuff," said Father.

"God kill me I should ever admit it!" said Mother.

"What I came in to say, was—" Father said, "I'm washing my hands of the whole business."

"You're always washing your hands," Mother said.

"It's no picnic," Father said. "You get a man in the house and the first thing you know you can't get him out."

"No such luck," Mother said.

"I'm warning you—" Father said.

"Tell your father he can go wash his hands!" Mother shouted.

"Eva—" Father said, "there is no need to shout."

"It's this damn house," Mother said. "Twenty-eight rooms and two babies. An old man, and two pretty babies."

"All right," said Father, "have your stroke."

"When I do—" Mother said, "I want someone here with me. 1 won't have a stroke and be cooped up here alone."

"Eva—" Father said, "that will be enough."

Mother let her long hair slip from her lap and stared at her front face in the mirror. Her mouth was open, and the new bridge was going up and down. She took the bridge out of her mouth and felt along the inside of her mouth with her finger. She spread her mouth wide with her fingers to see if she could see something.

"If you just keep it up," Father said, "you're going to have a little something—"

"Where's my baby?" Mother turned to look for Emily. She was sitting on the head of the polar bear feeding fern leaves to the rabbit. "If you do that he'll make bee-bees," Mother said. "You want him to go around the house making bee-bees?"

"It's not a him," said Robert, "it's a her."

33

"You have to shout?" shouted Father. "We're sitting right here."

"That's why *I* have to shout!" shouted Mother.

"Don't pick her up," Father said, "put her down. It's picking her up that makes bee-bees. If you don't want bee-bees pick her up by the ears."

Emily picks her up by the ears, then puts her down.

"I swear to God you're all crazy," Mother said. "Who could ever like that?"

Father takes his drink from the floor and holds it out toward Robert. There is a fly in it. "You see that?" Robert saw it. "What is it?"

"A fly," said Robert.

"Don't let him fool you, baby."

"Son—" said Father, "what kind of fly is it?"

"Are you crazy?" said Mother.

"Not so fast," said Father, "what kind of fly is it?"

"A drownded fly," said Robert.

"A drowned fly," said Father.

"Why should he look at a drowned fly?" said Mother.

Father didn't answer. He held the glass close to his face and blew on the fly as if to cool it. It rocked on the water but nothing happened.

"You would agree the fly is drowned?" his father asked.

"Don't agree to anything, baby."

"I'm going to hold this fly under water," said Father, "while you go and bring your father a saucer and a saltcellar."

"Don't you do it," said Mother.

"Obey your father," said Father.

Robert put his mother's hairpins in her lap and went back through the club room, the dining room, the game room, through the swinging door into the kitchen. Callie's metal saltcellar sat on the stove, where the heat kept it dry. He sprinkled some on the floor, crunched on it, then carried it back through the house to his father.

"Where's the saucer?" Father said.

"They're not for flies," said Mother. She took the ashtray from her dresser and passed it to Robert. Father used his silver pencil to push the fly to the edge of the glass, then fish it out. A drowned fly. It lay on its back, its wings stuck to the ashtray.

"This fly has been in the water twenty minutes," said Father. "That's a lot longer than your Mr. Brady."

"What did you drown him for?" asked Robert.

"I got the urge," said Father. "Cost me a drink!"

"It's probably a *her*," Mother said. "If it drowns, it's a her."

Father took the blotter from Mother's writing table and used one corner of it to pick up the fly. The drowned fly made a dark wet spot on the blotter. "Mumbo-jumbo, abracadabra—" chanted Father. "Your father will now bring the fly to life!" He put the blotter with the fly on the ashtray, then sprinkled the fly all over with salt. He kept sprinkling until the salt covered the fly like snow.

"My God, what next?" said Mother.

"It is now twenty-one minutes past five," said Father, and held out his watch so Robert could read it.

"Twenty-two minutes," said Robert.

"It was twenty-one when I started," said Father. "It was twenty-two when we had him covered. It takes a while for the magic to work."

"What magic?"

"Bringing the dead to life," said Father. He took one of Mother's cork-tipped cigarettes, lit it with her lighter, then swallowed the smoke.

"It's not coming out your ears," Emily said.

35

"That's another trick," said Father, "not this one." He swallowed more smoke, then he held the glowing tip of the cigarette very close to the fly. From where she sat Mother threw her brush at him and it skidded on the floor. "What we need is some light on the subject," said Father, "but more light than that." He looked around the room to the lamp Mother used to make her face brown. "Here we are," said Father, and pulled the lamp over. He held it so the green blotter and the salt were right beneath it. Robert could not see the fly. The brightness of the light made the green look blue. "Feel that!" said Father, and put his face beneath it.

"My God, you look like a turkey gobbler," Mother said.

"When you get my age—" Father began.

"What makes you think I'm going to get your age?" said Mother.

"Well, well—" Father said, "did you see it?"

"What?" said Robert.

"At sixty-two years of age," said Father, "I find my eye is sharper than yours. You know why?"

"Tell him your mother knows why," said Mother.

"You know why?" Father said. "I have trained myself to look out of the corner of my eye. Out of the corner we can detect the slightest movement. With the naked eye we can pick up the twitch of a fly."

"How your father's taste has changed!" cried Mother.

Up through the salt, like the limb of a snowman, appeared the leg of the fly. "Look! Look!" cried Robert.

"Four minutes and twenty seconds," said Father. "Brought him around in less time than it took to drown him." The fly used his long rear legs like poles to clean off the snow. Using his naked eyes just like Father, Robert could see the hairs on the legs, like brushes. He used them like dusting crumbs from the table. He

36

began to wash off his face, like a cat. "Five minutes and forty seconds so far," said Father.

"Does he know who he is?" asked Robert.

"The salt soaked up the water," said Father, and used the silver pencil to tip the fly to his feet. The fly buzzed but didn't fly anywhere. He buzzed like he felt trapped.

"How many times can he do it?" said Robert.

"A good healthy fly," said Father, "can probably come back four or five times."

"Don't he get tired?" Robert said.

"You get tired of anything," Father said, and picked up the fly, dropped him back into the drink. He just lay there, floating on the top. He didn't buzz.

"He's pooped," said Emily.

"Pooped?" said Father. "Where did she hear that?" Mother was looking at her face close to the mirror. Father pushed the fly under the water but he didn't buzz. "No reaction," said Father. He put the glass and the ashtray on Mother's dresser. "He's probably an old fly," Father said, "it probably wasn't the first time somebody dunked him."

"What's that?" Mother said. There was a flapping around from the direction of the game room.

"You leave the screen up, son?" Father said. When Robert left the screens up bats flew into the house because it was dark. They had flown so close to Robert the wind of their wings ruffled his hair. Her golden hair fanned out on her shoulders, Mother went to the hall door and threw it open. The flapping sound stopped.

"Callie!" Mother called, "is that you, Callie?"

"You crazy?" said Father. "Her lungs are full of water. She almost drowned."

"What a lunch!" said Mother. "You ever see anything like it? If I know her she just won't stand it."

37

There was a wheezing sound, then suddenly music. Through the dark beyond his mother, across the tile floored room, Robert could see the keys of the piano playing.

"My God, it's him!" said Mother. "It's the lover!"

Father got up from the bed and put the robe with the dragons around her shoulders. He used both hands to lift her hair from inside it. Mother crossed the hall, her robe tassels dragging, to where the cracked green blinds were drawn at the windows. "You poor darling!" she cried, jerking on the blind cords. "How can you see in the dark?" When the blind zipped up Robert could see the lover sitting on the bench at the player piano. His legs pumped. He gripped the sides of the bench so he wouldn't slip off. He wore his hat but his laces were untied and slapped the floor when he pumped.

"Now how'd he get in *there*?" said Father. "How explain that?"

"Go right on pumping," Mother said, "play as long as you like." She stooped to read the label on the empty roll box. " 'The Barcarolle'! Imagine!"

"It's not," said Robert.

"I'd like to have it explained," Father said. "The only closed-up room in the house."

"It's not the 'Barcarolle,' " said Robert.

"I know, baby," said Mother. She stood with the empty roll box at the verandah window looking at the lovers' statue in the bird bath. Kissing. One of her orioles splashed them. Across the pond there were cars parked in Mrs. Van Zant's driveway and some of the Japanese lanterns were glowing.

"If only she was here to hear it," Mother said.

Robert said, "She likes it better when you play it backwards."

"If only she was here to see it!" Mother said.

"She's seen it every summer since the war," said Father.

"Oh no you don't," said Mother. "It's just once you see it."

38

"Now you see it, now you don't, eh?" said Father. He rubbed his palms together. "When do we eat? Guess I'll go wash my hands."

Mr. Brady, the lover, sat in the covered wicker chair with the paper napkin and the plate in his lap. He wore his hat. He sat looking at Mrs. Van Zant's Japanese lanterns. Out on the pond was a boy in a red inner tube, splashing. Mrs. Van Zant's husband walked around beneath the lanterns, screwing in bulbs. . .

"All right, all right," Mother said, "but I'm not going to sit on these iron chairs."

"There were your prescription," Father said.

"Not to sit on." Mother spread her napkin on the floor, sat on it. She spread her golden hair on the wicker chair arm.

"Listen to this," Father said, "rain tonight and tomorrow morning. Turning cool late tonight with moderately cool westerly winds." Father wet his finger and put up his hand. "South westerly," he said.

"Tell your father how we need him," Mother said.

"What about his h-a-t," Father said.

"Don't you think he can s-p-e-l-l?" said Robert.

"Your father never takes anything for granted," Mother said.

"I don't want him forming habits," Father said, "that he's going to find hard to break when he's better."

"I don't think he's hungry," Mother said. "He's thinking about her. I know it."

"Asked him if he'd like a drink. Said he doesn't drink. Asked him if he'd like to smoke. Said he doesn't smoke."

"What's your father mumbling now?"

"A man has to do something—" Father said.

"Which would you rather be—" said Robert, "a rabbit or a

39

hare?"

The lover stood up and spilled his pizza on the floor.

"You can just go and get me another plate," Mother said, and gave the lover the one she was holding. He sat down in the chair and held it in his lap.

"Asked him if he played rummy. He shook his head. Asked him if he played bridge. He shook his head. Suppose you ask him if he can do anything."

"Tell your father how we love him," Mother said.

"I don't care what his field is," Father said, "whether it's stocks and bonds, insurance, or religion. It doesn't matter what it is, a man has to do something. Smoke, drink, play the ponies—he has to do *some*thing."

"I have never heard a sorrier confession," Mother said.

Robert sang—

*Star light, star bright*
*First star I seen tonight*

"Wouldn't that be *saw*?" Father said.

"SSSShhhhhhh—" said Mother. Across the lake Mrs. Van Zant's loudspeaker was saying something. Mrs. Van Zant's voice came across the water, the people clapped, the drummer beat his drums. More of the Japanese lanterns came on.

"If I don't love the Orient," Mother said.

"You didn't when we were there," Father said. The drummer beat his drums, stopped, and the music played.

"How old is Sylvia now?" Mother said.

"You don't know?" said Father, "or you don't want to know? She's your first one, right? That makes her fifteen this summer."

"I don't know as it matters," Mother said. "The right time is whenever it happens. Heaven knows I was just a little fool when it happened to me."

"I wasn't so smart myself," Father said.

"If my mother had been like some people," Mother said, "she would have locked me in the bedroom, or shipped me off to Boston, or some place like that to a boarding school. But she *knew*— she knew the right time is whenever it happens."

"You talking to me, by chance?" Father said.

"I can honestly say—" Mother said, "I knew what it was the minute I saw her. I knew what it was the minute she came in the house. I knew what it was—I felt the whole business all over again."

"Just what's going on here?" Father said.

Robert jumped up from the steps and ran into the trees. He ran up and down, back and forth, up and down. He ran around and around the lovers in the bird bath. He stopped running and sang—

> *Beans, beans, the musical fruit*
> *The more you eat, the more you toot.*

"You hear that?" said Father.

"Baby—" Mother said, "we don't sing songs like that."

"I feel it—" Robert said. "I feel it—I feel it!"

"I know, baby," Mother said, "but we don't sing it."

"WHY?" Robert shouted.

"It doesn't show your breeding," Mother said.

Robert stopped jumping up and down and looked across the lake. The Japanese lanterns were waving and the colors were on the water. The music played.

"Time for Amos and Andy," Father said. The music stopped. A man sang—

*The moon was all aglow*
*And the devil was in your eyes.*

"Fifteen is fifteen—" Mother said.

"Robert is eight!" Robert said, and ran up and down, up and down, up and down. The man sang—

*How deep is the o-shun*
*How high is the skyyyy*
*How great my de-voshun*
*I'll tell you no lie—*

"You ever hear anything like that?" said Father.

"Let it happen when it happens," Mother said, "and whatever else, they can't take it from you." Mother laughed.

Father stood up and walked to the edge of the porch. "You want to make yourself sick? Stop that fool running. You've just had your supper." Robert ran into the woods and hid. He hid behind the lovers kissing and peeked at the house. "If you people will excuse me—" Father said, and went inside. He walked down the hardwood floor and turned the radio on, loud.

"You want to be foolish, too?" Mother said.

"No—" Emily said.

"Go be foolish anyhow," Mother said, so Emily ran from the porch and around the sprinkler on the lawn. She ran through the sprinkler and into the trees and splashed her hands in the bird bath, splashing the lovers, splashing Robert in the face. Robert chased her back and forth on the lawn. Robert chased her through the trees, through the garden weeds, and down the cinder path to the pier. He chased her out on the pier and caught her out on the diving board. "Let go of me, you beast!" she said. He let her go.

"What are they doing?" he said.

"They are kissing," she said.

"They are not kissing!" he said.

"They are lovers!" she said, and almost pushed him into the water. Then she ran down the pier and into the grove, around and around the lovers with him behind her, until he caught her and smeared the fresh green slime in her hair. Then they ran around and around the lovers, around the sprinkler, around the verandah, until he caught her and they wrestled in the weeds. They stopped wrestling and lay quiet, listening. The man sang—

*I walked into an April shower*
*I stepped into an open door*
*I found a million dollar baby*
*In the five and ten cent stoooore*

"Ba-by—" Mother said. "Oh ba-by, come and play us something."

"See—" she said, and Robert rolled over, spit in her hair. Then he got up and ran around the house.

The light was on in the music room. From the steps of the verandah he could see the gold fish bowl, the fairy castle, the lamp with the marble base, and the golden braid tassels on the shade. Beyond the lamp he could see part of the lover in the wicker chair.

"You like it fast or you like it slow?" Robert said.

"We like it slow," Mother said, and Robert moved the lever. He held on to the bench and played *Isle Of My Golden Dreams*. He played it forward, slow, then he played it backwards, fast.

"Don't get in your mother's hair, pet—" Mother said.

Robert played *Officer Of The Day*. He played it forward, fast, then he played it backwards, very slow.

"They're playing your song, baby—" Mother said. "Listen to the man singing your song." The man sang—

> *You're the cream in my coffee*
> *You're the salt in my stew*
> *You will always be*
> *My ne-cess-ity*
> *I'd be lost without youuuuu*

When the man stopped singing, Robert played *William Tell*. He played it backwards, very, very slow.

"Oh Ralph—!" Mother said, "will you speak to your son?" Robert played *It's A Long Way To Tipperary,* forward and backwards very fast. Mother came in from the verandah and knocked on the folding doors. She tried the folding doors but they wouldn't move.

"You said those doors didn't work," Father said. Father was sitting at his desk with his eye shade on. He was looking through his magnifying glass at some of his stamps. Mother kicked on the doors. "Now there's no need to get excited—" Father said. Mother went around through the club room and tried the other door.

"Will you unlock this door?" Mother said. Robert played very loud. "Baby—" Mother said, "you know what your mother is going to do?" "Son—" Father said, "You hear what your Mother said?"

"You know what Mother's going to do? All right—" she said, "we'll see who likes to be locked in. We'll see who's best at this business of being locked in." Mother went back through the club room, the dining room, and across the hall to her own bedroom door. She opened the door, went in, turned the key in the lock. They could hear her slam the doors to the garden, turn the keys

44

in the locks.

"Now you see what you've done?" Father said. "You know what you are doing to your Mother?" Father pounded on the door.

"Tell your father to please go away," Mother said.

"Go to your Mother," Father said to Robert. "Your Mother is not well. Go to your Mother." So he went back through the club room, and the dining room, and knocked at Mother's door.

"It's me, Mother—" he said. Mother opened the door and let him in. She kicked her shoes off and went back and lay down on the bed. "You love your Mother?"

"Yes, Mother—"

"Yes, Mother, yes Mother, yes Mother, yes Mother, yes Mother," his mother said.

"Oh Eva—?" his Father said.

"Your father has the brains of a fish," Mother said.

"I got him stopped," Father said. "You hear? I got him stopped."

"Jabber, jabber, jabber, jabber, jabber—" said Mother.

"He's stopped," Father said. "Why don't you just relax."

"Why don't I have a stroke?" Mother said "Why don't I have a stroke and let you spoon feed me?"

"You're distraught," Father said.

"It's a plain simple question," Mother said. "You're a great one for plain simple questions."

"I wash my hands—" Father said, rubbing his palms.

"For the love of mud," said Mother, "go away!"

Father went away. Mother got up from the bed and took a seat on the stool where she had three faces in the mirrors. She put on jar number One and rubbed it in with her fingers. She looked at what she had done and wiped it off with tissue. She put on jar number Two, in big thick gobs, and just let it run.

45

As if he was outside and wanted in Robert said, "Knock, knock, knock."

"Yes, love," said Mother.

Robert put out his fists and said, "Which hand do you take?"

Mother looked at him in one of her mirrors. "You wouldn't fool your mother, baby?"

"Go on, choose," said Robert.

Mother turned on the stool to look at his fists, one green with slime.

"Pollywogs again!"

"You got to choose," he said.

Mother closed her eyes and chose his clean fist. She opened her eyes and looked at what he held in his palm.

"Sugar? Ain't I sweet enough, baby?"

"Why don't you taste it," he said, "it's not sugar."

She held his palm close to her face, sniffed at it, then flicked her tongue at it.

"Salt!" she shouted. "What does your mother want with salt?"

Robert just stood there with the salt in his palm.

At the door Father said, "You two have to shout? I'm going to take him for a walk. Little walk to the village. He's got to do something. The only thing left for him to do is to walk."

Father went away. Through the French doors his mother looked across the pond at the Japanese lanterns and the people dancing. The music came in. Mother said, "That one. What's that?"

"It's not the 'Barcarolle,' " said Robert. Mother picked up her brush and stroked it slowly through her golden hair. The electricity crackled. It would lift from her shoulders to be near the brush.

"Do something for your mother, baby." He waited to see what it was. "Go sprinkle it on your father," she said and turned to give him a hug.

A FIGHT BETWEEN A WHITE BOY AND A BLACK
BOY IN THE DUSK OF A FALL AFTERNOON IN
OMAHA, NEBRASKA

How did it start? If there is room for speculation, it lies in how to end it. Neither the white boy nor the black boy gives it further thought. They stand, braced off, in the cinder-covered schoolyard, in the shadow of the darkened red brick building. Eight or ten smaller boys circle the fighters, forming sides. A white boy observes the fight upside down as he hangs by his knees from the iron rail of the fence. A black girl pasting cutouts of pumpkins in the windows of the annex seems unconcerned. Fights are not so unusual. Halloween and pumpkins come but once a year.

At the start of the fight there was considerable jeering and exchange of formidable curses. The black boy was much better at this part of the quarrel and jeered the feebleness of his opponent's remarks. The white boy lacked even the words. His experience with taunts and scalding invective proved to be remarkably shallow. Twice the black boy dropped his arms as if they were useless against such a potato-mouthed, stupid adversary. Once he laughed, showing the coral roof of his mouth. In the shadow of the school little else stood out clearly for the white boy to strike at. The black boy did not have large whites to his eyes, or pearly white teeth. In the late afternoon light he made a poor target except for the shirt that stood out against the fence that closed in the school. He had rolled up the sleeves and opened the collar so that he could breathe easier and fight better. His black bare feet are the exact color of the cinder yard.

The white boy is a big hulking fellow, large for his age. It is not clear what it might be, since he has been in the same grade for three years. The bottom board has been taken from the drawer of his desk to allow for his knees. Something said about that may have started the quarrel, or the way he likes to suck on toy train wheels. (He blows softly and wetly through the hole, the wheel at the front of his mouth.) But none of that is clear; all that is known is that he stands like a boxer, his head ducked low, his huge fists doubled before his face. He stands more front-ally than sidewise, as if uncertain which fist to lead with. As a rule he wrestles. He would much rather wrestle than fight with his fists. Perhaps he refused to wrestle with a black boy, and *that* could be the problem. One never knows. Who ever knows for sure what starts a fight?

The black boy's age hardly matters and it doesn't show. All that shows clearly is his shirt and the way he stands. His head looks small because his shoulders are so wide. He has seen pictures of famous boxers and stands with his left arm stretched out before him as if approaching something in the darkness. His right arm, cocked, he holds as if his chest pained him. Both boys are hungry, scared, and waiting for the other one to give up.

The white boy is afraid of the other one's blackness, and the black boy hates and fears whiteness. Something of their mutual fear is now shared by those who are watching. One of the small black boys hoots like an Indian and takes off. One of the white boys has a pocketful of marbles he dips his hand into and rattles. This was distracting when the fight first started, and he was asked to take his hands out of his pockets. Now it eases the strain of the silence.

The need to take sides has also dwindled, and the watchers have gathered with the light behind them, out of their eyes. They say "Come on!" the way you say "sic 'em," not caring which dog.

50

A pattern has emerged which the two fighters know, but it is not yet known to the watchers. Nobody is going to win. The dilemma is how nobody is going to lose. It has early been established that the black boy will hit the white boy on the head with a sound like splitting a melon—but it's the white boy who moves forward, the black boy who moves back. It isn't clear if the white boy, or any of the watchers, perceives the method in this tactic. Each step backward the black boy takes he is closer to home, and nearer to darkness.

In time they cross the cinder-covered yard to the narrow steps going down to the sidewalk. There the fight is delayed while a passing adult, a woman with a baby sitting up in its carriage, tells them to stop acting like children, and asks their names to inform their teachers. The black boy's name is Eustace Beecher. The white boy's name is Emil Hrdlic, or something like that. He's a real saphead, and not at all certain how it is spelled. When the woman leaves, they return to their fighting and go along the fronts of darkened houses. Dogs bark. Little dogs, especially, enjoy a good fight.

The black boy has changed his style of fighting so that his bleeding nose doesn't drip on his shirt. The white boy has switched around to give his cramped, cocked arm a rest. The black boy picks up support from the fact that he doesn't take advantage of this situation. One reason might be that his left eye is almost closed. When he stops to draw a shirtsleeve across his face, the white boy does not leap forward and strike him. It's a good fight. They have learned what they can do and what they can't do.

At the corner lit up by the bug-filled street lamp they lose about half of their seven spectators. It's getting late and dark. You can smell the bread baking on the bakery draft. The light is better for the fighters now than the watchers, who see the two figures only in profile. It's not so easy anymore to see which one is black and which one is white. Sometimes the black boy, out of habit, takes a step backward, then has to hop forward to his proper position. The hand he thrusts out before him is limp at the wrist, as if he had just dropped something unpleasant. The white boy's shirt, once blue in color, shines like a slicker on his sweaty back. The untied laces of his shoes are broken from the way he is always stepping on them. He is the first to turn his head and check the time on the bakery clock.

Behind the black boy the street enters the Negro section. Down there, for two long blocks, there is no light. A gas street lamp can be seen far at the end, the halo around it swimming with insects. One of the two remaining fight watchers whistles shrilly, then enters the bakery to buy penny candy. There's a gum-ball machine that sometimes returns your penny, but it takes time, and you have to shake it.

The one spectator left to watch this fight stands revealed in the glow of the bakery window. One pocket is weighted with marbles; the buckles of his britches are below his knees. He watches the fighters edge into the darkness where the white shirt of the black boy is like an object levitated at a séance. Nothing else can be seen. Black boy and white boy are swallowed up. For a moment one can hear the shuffling feet of the white boy; then that, too, dissolves into darkness. The street is a tunnel with a lantern gleaming far at its end. The last fight watcher stands as if paralyzed until the rumble of a passing car can be felt through the soles of his shoes, tingling the blood in his feet. Behind him the glow of the sunset reddens the sky. He goes toward it on the run, a racket of marbles, his eyes fixed on the "FORD" sign beyond the school building, where there is a hollow with a shack used by ice skaters under which he can crawl and peer out like a cat. When the street lights cast more light he will go home.

Somewhere, still running, there is a white boy who saw all of this and will swear to it; otherwise, nothing of what he saw remains. The Negro section, the bakery on the corner, the red brick school with one second-floor window (the one that opens out on the fire escape) outlined by the chalk dust where they slapped the erasers—all of that is gone, the earth levelled and displaced to accommodate the ramps of the new freeway. The cloverleaf approaches look great from the air. It saves the driving time of those headed east or west. Omaha is no longer the gateway to the West, but the plains remain, according to one traveller, a place where his wife still sleeps in the seat while he drives through the night.

FIONA

In England, where Fiona felt free, she would tie the sleeves of a sweater about her waist, fill the pockets of her tunic with Fig Newtons, then clop for hours through a landscape green as the sea and almost as wet. She loved the pelt of rain on her hair, the splatter of it on her face. This rain did not pour. It hung like a vapor that settled on her skin and smoked in her lungs. Trotting and walking, the drizzle steaming her face, her legs sliced with the drag and tangle of the grass, those who heard her coming or going said that she sounded like a winded horse. How that made her laugh! From these wet runs she would return to her room soaked to the skin, too exhausted to sleep, like one of the small watery cubs of Beowulf's dam, escaped from the deep. That's her own description. The one subject she never tires of is herself.

Time would prove that nothing else would arouse in Fiona such a full awareness of her flesh as a piece of nature. Sex didn't. In her opinion, strange as it seems, there was too much in sex that was *im*material. All of the sentiment, for one thing. Then all of the mess. Fiona didn't blather it to the world, but she took for *granted* the primacy of the spirit. That seemed obvious. The difficult and the beautiful thing was to make the spirit flesh. That common practice would see it just the other way around was a flaw in man, not in nature, and the major flaw in man—she would add with a guffaw—was the one she had married. A joke? That was how people took it. Including Charles, the one she had married. Fiona's strident, horsey laugh is surprising in a woman

57

of her cultivation. Seated, she rocks back and forth, slapping her knees. One sees the teeth she has missing and the dark cave at the back of her mouth. So the gods must laugh at men, and in the same spirit Fiona laughs at the gods. Who else can be held responsible? On their last trip to the coast (they took a Pullman) the porter had assumed that the man along with her, in his cap and sports jacket, *had* to be her son. What could she do but laugh? She had learned to live with it, but what she found a strain was how his weakness seemed to give him strength. Life clung to him. He lacked even the strength to fight it off. Every day of her life it was forced upon Fiona that this hapless man she had married would survive her. The older he became the younger he looked. If he wore his tennis sneakers and went out without his hat, students at the college took him for an instructor. Some of the girls swooned to learn that he read Greek. With a few exceptions, only Fiona could appreciate the humor of her situation, the love of folly being the last, great love of her life.

Somehow the first question Fiona is asked is where in the world, and how, she met Charles. Why will take time. It is not felt necessary to ask where in the world Charles met Fiona. Perhaps he didn't. It is obvious that Fiona met him. This question is a natural at the yearly fall parties introducing new members of the department. Fiona, who is pouring tea, will be seated. Charles stands—somehow he is always standing—an erect, handsome man, scholarly, cultivated, his face little changed from the day Fiona met him thirty years ago. That can't be, of course, but it is. Charles wears caps, does not wear glasses unless he sits reading, has the attractive smattering of grey hair of a young college man. No wrinkles. A seam where his head joins his neck. He stands, thighs pressed together, holding in one cupped palm an elbow, in the other a silver-rimmed glass with three ice cubes and his first stint of daily bourbon. If any, the water comes from the ice. If

witty and effusive, Charles is tight, and capable of a very mis-
leading performance. His manner, and the Oxford accent that
time has not eroded, lead people to correctly think that Fiona
met him in England. It is never easy for them to accept that
Charles was born in Indiana, just thirty miles north of Pickett,
where he attended a school so backward he was able to major in
Greek. This had more than a little to do with his being chosen as
a Rhodes scholar; being chosen by Fiona shortly followed. They
were married in France.

Charles will go on to tell you—if Fiona hasn't—that in his
second year at Oxford, on a walking tour with a companion, he
stopped to watch two teams of girls club each other nearly sense-
less. The game was lacrosse. The most proficient clubber of the
lot was Fiona. But at that very moment she was getting hers with
a sharp crack on the elbow: for the cello (she planned a career in
music) she exchanged Charles, as simple as that. Broad in the
shoulders and hips, long-limbed and large-boned, a mane of chest-
nut hair in two pigtails, Fiona Copley personified the spirit of
Sparta that seemed to be absent from the study of the classics.
There is a snapshot of Charles, taken on that excursion, standing
just to one side of the Amazon, Fiona, that sums up in a glance
the new world that is born, and the world that is gone. His arms
are folded on his chest. His finger marks the place in a book of
Housman's poems. If Housman's brook proved too broad for
leaping, it was not entirely Charles's decision. At the sound of the
word "leap," he had leaped. Was it at that moment he first ex-
perienced, or suffered, Fiona's laugh? Uninhibited, laced with
fragments of what she happens to be chewing, it is not now, nor
was it then, unusual for Fiona to almost choke to death. The only
cure is several thumps, with the flat of the hand, on her broad
back. Both friends and colleagues not so friendly have had oc-
casion to thump Fiona. She takes it in good spirits. It often starts

her laughing again. Flushed with coughing, her face red and per-spiring, she will glance up at Charles, who stands tunelessly whistling, or toying with one of the cubes in his drink.

"I believe he'd let me choke rather than thump me!" she will cry, and this often leads to another fit of coughing. It is the truth that makes Fiona laugh, never mind what it is.

Neither a pretty girl nor a womanly woman—even her abund-ant hair is like a barrister's wig—Fiona resembles a well-endowed but obvious female impersonator. Her feet are large, her strides are that of Piers Plowman in foot-molded shoes. If she came at the wrong time, and in the wrong country, nevertheless she came to the right school. Her music festivals attract the gifted, fussy people who consider Aspen too high, Lucerne too far, and the Berkshires too close. They have precisely the taste and quaint cultivated madness to enjoy Charles's slides of the Crusader castles, a subject on which they will admit him to be the author-ity. For thirty-one years he has been at work on the text. It can be idly examined in the whiskey cartons that line one wall of his study: they stack well, and he can always assume they contain something else. Scholarly books in Greek and Latin, bound in vellum, stuffed like wallets with cards and notations, occupy the table, the chairs, and the bed where Charles does his sleeping and reading. Every year, for twelve years, a scholarly press adver-tised the book and took orders for it, then announced a brief de-lay in its publication. Some scholars hold the opinion the work is published, but hard to find. The work keeps him happy. More important, it keeps him out of the way. Fiona has a lively interest in people, and will sometimes say that she *collects* men. Their wives are always told there is no reason to worry, and they don't.

Before settling down Fiona and Charles had lived everywhere one could do it cheaply. Majorca first, of course, and then the Costa Brava. After Ibiza to Rhodes, where Charles continued his exhaustive researches into Crusader castles, and from there to Corfu, to Mykonos, to Dubrovnik, then to Minorca and the Canaries, a winter in Madeira, and several summers island-hopping, in and out of known and unknown villas on which Fiona left the impression of royalty in exile. This characteristic had the effect of enlarging her past and diminishing her future. It was seldom asked where she was off to—merely where she had been. The whack on the elbow had scotched a career, but it could hardly be said it ruined her talent. On an income of less than three thousand a year, with introductions to people who sat waiting for them, they managed to be warm when it was freezing and reasonably cool when it was stifling, living with people but not strictly off them, and always remarkably independent. In those years the London office of the Oxford Press—with other offices in Bombay, Calcutta, and elsewhere—received further material on a volume that would be definitive if it was ever completed.

No matter what island, Charles was up early, Fiona slept late. Her quality showed to its greatest advantage in her mastery of leisure. She detested committees, cultivated no hobbies, and showed no interest in world- or self-improvement. Charles did his writing in the morning, and after lunch they would take a long walk together: their hosts impatiently waited for the clop of their hobbled boots on the porch. Both wore hiking shoes, carried binoculars, canes, biscuits, and bars of bitter Swiss chocolate. Chocolate kept Fiona going as she waited for Charles to determine where.

On their honeymoon—a walking tour of the Alps—Fiona had insisted on visiting the tiny village of Coppet, noted as the burial place of Madame de Staël. That seemed understandable. Fiona had much in common with a woman of her temperament and talents. Charles knew the usual things about Madame de Staël but he had not heard the story about her mother, Madame Necker.

61

She did not have her daughter's assortment of talents, nor did she dream, like her daughter, of an enduring fame. Yet she had her dream. In some respects a very ambitious one. Madame Necker did not want to *live* forever, but she did want to survive. Not in the hearts and minds of men, like her child, but in the sweet solid flesh of her own bones. Death she did not fear. Physical disintegration she did. To die she was willing—to turn to food for worms she was not. Over the years she had observed, like many people, that actual bodies were preserved in large stoppered bottles, where they floated in the clear, immortal broth of alcohol. If this could be done for God's smaller creatures, why not for a large one like Madame Necker? All one needed was a bottle, or a cask, big enough. So she had one made, a huge glass-lined cask large enough for both Madame Necker and her husband. It was filled with alcohol. Soon enough, it floated the remains of the Neckers, and by draining off an appropriate quantity of the liquid room was made, in time, for Madame de Staël. It was this excess liquid —according to tradition, and as recounted to Charles by Fiona— that was used to fortify the local vintage, and make it much in demand.

On such a story such a twist was to be expected, but who could guess that Fiona would never tire of it? Nor did her listeners, the way she could tell it. It often left her gasping and choking, tears of laughter in her eyes. Only Charles, who lacked Fiona's strong stomach, seemed to be a little sensitive about it. His comment was that the story betrayed her original but somewhat perverse ancestral worship. She had replied that it was no such thing: it was pure self-love. Nor was she the first to cherish the fat of her own bones. Self-love seemed to Fiona—as she never tired of saying— much less perverse than other forms of love with which she was familiar, a comment that diverted the discussion to other things.

I need to emphasize that Fiona's self-love has little to do with matters of the spirit. She is the first to point out that the spirit is free to shift for itself—it's her too solid flesh that gives her the willies. Into dust or worse? She won't accept it. The important point is, she no longer has to. All of that is part of the past—one large past—that she has put behind her. The discovery and perfection of the modern freezing unit—at about the time she was at school in England—made it possible for Fiona to be practical as well as ambitious. Survival in the flesh was no problem. The problems now were in the field of thawing out.

This obsession—or passion, if you prefer it—has its origin in her childhood. One winter Fiona, with her brother Ronald, skated on a millpond near the house. It's still there: one of many nuisances she refuses to give up. The first freeze of winter had left the pond ice clear as glass. Fiona didn't skate too well, as a child, and spent most of the time on her hands and knees, peering into the ice. On that day she saw, just a few inches beneath her, the wide staring eyes of a life-size doll, frozen in the ice. The lips were parted. She felt it might speak back if she spoke to it. She called to her brother and they stood there considering how to get the doll out of the ice. Ronald ran to the house, and returned with a sled and a saw that his father used to remove blocks of ice in the spring. After a great deal of effort they lugged the block home on Ronald's sled. As the ice quickly thawed in a tub of warm water the doll's lovely hair spread out on the surface. A moment later Fiona was able to free one of the chubby pink hands. Ronald says that she shrieked like a wild bird at the touch. This doll's hand was that of a recently drowned child. It had been so perfectly preserved in the ice that Fiona believed it must still be alive. It took time to convince her. She was convinced that it merely slept, and would speak to her when it thawed. The thaw, unfortunately, soon occurred, and she watched the flawlessly beautiful eyes dissolve like ice cubes and run down the cheeks like tears.

Such an experience is not easily forgotten. For a child like Fiona it was crucial. It provided her, as she admits herself, with the key to her own nature. Survival was what she wanted: survival in the flesh. This bizarre experience had revealed to her how it might be done.

For Charles, the crucial revelation was his brief acquaintance with Madame Necker, floating in the huge cask in Coppet. There he saw for himself how well alcohol preserved the flesh. He accepted the proof, but preferred to take it internally. When the time came to die he would be so well pickled he would require only framing.

As it applied to Charles, Fiona came to be fond of the word *pickled*. Charles is pickled, she would say, to explain his occasional absence, or the way he might stand, the glass cupped in his palm, blowing softly on the ice cubes as if to thaw them, a dimpled, archaic smile on his moist lips.

For all her love of alcohol, Fiona does not drink. Neither does she smoke, but for years her health has not been good. Her hair is white, several joints are stiffening, and there will soon be little flesh to preserve on the bones.

For all that he drinks, Charles's health appears to be good. He is one of those men who seem to be preserved in the very liquid that destroys so many others. His teeth are white. He has a thick pelt of hair. True enough, he does have the shakes, which is why he holds the glass in such a curious manner, the cubes tinkling as he stands like a good whiskey ad with his back to the fire. It is one thing to be pickled, briefly, while alive: quite another to be pickled, and bottled, forever. It's the *forever* that bugs him, and helps explain his apparent good health.

To have nothing to fear but fear itself, Charles will tell you, is more than sufficient. For one thing, pure fear is inexhaustible.

For another, the age has caught up with Charles, after so long being safely behind him. Once only alcohol would preserve what seemed to matter. Now there is dry ice. It took a few thousand years and great quantities of ice to preserve the woolly mammoth in the wastes of Siberia, but this could currently be done at small expense in a frozen-food locker. It is Fiona's idea that a huge floating freezer would have served much better than Noah's ark. In the freezer, two of every kind of creature would still be as fresh as the day they were frozen, with a more than fifty-fifty chance to be thawed and put back into circulation. In the basement of her home Fiona has her own freezer, one six feet six inches long and forty inches wide. That is large enough for her: to prove it she will stretch out in it for you, the metallic walls of the box magnifying her remarkably resonant laughter. Does she plan on just lying there forever? Why not? Just in case the power might go off during an electric storm, or an air raid, she has installed a power plant that operates on its own gasoline motor. Charles—who still looks as young as ever—will be around to supervise and keep things going. If by chance he isn't, the box is also large enough for him. One of her expanding programs, now gathering members, is concerned with continued Freezer Survival, and will supply the organization and funds necessary to keep the current flowing. Everybody knows the idea of his dying first is what keeps Charles looking so young. Fiona makes him nervous, but he is the one with the black head of hair, she with the white one. Charles has the air of breeding that makes it unnecessary for him to talk very much. He stands a good deal, his back to the fireplace, or moves about whatever room he is in looking for new or old timepieces. He has a thing about clocks. Battery-driven ones interest him less than those activated by atmospheric pressure, or run by weights. The ticking that many find so aggravating appeals to Charles. He likes the modern clocks with the visible movements, or the older type with the pendulum rocking, perhaps a smaller dial on the face notching off the seconds. Time. What the devil is it?—Charles will ask. Since everybody knows he is a student of the subject the question is rhetorical, to say the least. It is a fiction, surely, having no meaning beyond the measurement of the past. Otherwise it is merely a form of the future tense. That simple, ticking hand of the clock indicates something that defies comprehension. Something that never was, for a moment is, and is as suddenly gone. In Fiona, for example, time ticks away in a visible, even audible, measure. In Charles, oddly enough, it appears to have stopped. An illusion, of course, as the beat of his heart can be seen in the tremor of his hand, or, when he is seated, in the wagging toe of his boot. If time is not the movement of one thing or another, has it stopped? If, indeed, a low point of freezing brings all movement to a standstill, can it be said, or proven, that time exists? Queries like that get from Fiona one of her memorable, infectious guffaws. The erosion of time can be seen at both the back and front of her mouth. Doesn't she care? She behaves like a player with the trump card. For all of her remarkable talents she sometimes seems a little simpleminded. Or on the mad side—whichever side that is. The latitude in these matters merely points up what we know to be the gist of the problem. On a subject of interest, of life and death, does anybody really know anything of importance? Just who is dying, for example, is as hard to determine as who is living. It is in the courts. We no longer know for sure when a person is dead.

Three days ago, now, Charles was found lying face up in the freezer as if he had dropped there. He was frozen stiff. That is all that can be said for certain: he is frozen stiff. Fiona will not allow the authorities to thaw him out. The one thing that is known for certain in these matters is that you can't refreeze what has once been thawed, and this is neither the time nor the place to bring Charles back for interrogation. If a better world was what he had in mind, this is not it.

Something will have to be done, sooner or later, but Fiona has threatened to sue for murder any person or persons who thaw Charles out. Until he is thawed, who can say what remains to be said? There is another school of thought on the matter, which suggests a period of watchful waiting. Why not? There is little or nothing that can happen to Charles. Ten years from now he will still be as he is. The authorities have adopted the position of watch and wait. Some believe it safe to assume, from her present appearance, that Fiona will not long survive him, and at the time of her death such legal steps as are found necessary might be taken. She is the one who laughs when she considers what they might be. I could be wrong, of course, but my impression is that Fiona is looking better than ever, now that Charles—that is, his future—has been taken care of. She looks younger. With a little persuasion she will join you in a drink.

IN ANOTHER COUNTRY

Madrid was so dim and sulfurous with smog that Carolyn wrote letters to five museum directors, urging them to save the paintings in the Prado while there was still time. Paintings were what Carolyn had come to see, but she actually found it hard with her eyes smarting, her sinuses clogged. Ralph had come to Spain to see Ronda, where they had once planned to honeymoon. Ralph had stumbled on it in Hemingway's bull book as the place a man should go when he bolted with a woman. They had not bolted, but Ralph had always wondered what they had missed, so now they would see. They took a plane to Seville, rented a car, and the same day drove to Arcos de la Frontera, a place hardly on the map but so fabulous Carolyn didn't want to leave. Wasn't it a commonplace that people didn't know when to *stop?* Carolyn did, and she had the premonition that after Arcos, anything would be a letdown. They might not have gone on, Carolyn feeling the way she did, if there had been a room for them in Arcos, but the small *parador* was full of English dames from the nineteenth century, one, surely, from the eighteenth century, who received their advice and encouragement through a tuba-shaped ear horn. A room had been found at a nearby resort, put up in a rush to meet the tourist traffic, the cabins so new the paint seemed sticky, and the sheets on their beds actually proved to be damp.

Carolyn had nearly died, and to keep her from freezing they shared a bed no larger than a cot. Moored at the pier on the artificial lake was a miniature paddle-wheel steamboat, with the word

"Mississippi" painted on the prow. It had been too much. Nevertheless, once they were up and had had breakfast, Carolyn had this feeling that Ronda would disappoint them, the view from Arcos being one that nothing could top. Why didn't they just act smart for once and fly to Barcelona and see the Gaudis? Even Ralph liked the Gaudis, or anything you couldn't get into a museum. Why didn't they compromise, Ralph said, and go to Barcelona if Ronda let them down? They might, anyway, if Carolyn's chill turned out to be a cold, which she would rather come down with in Barcelona where they had the name of an American dentist. Whenever they traveled, she lost fillings and gained weight.

A windless spring day, their drive to Ronda was so fabulous it made them both apprehensive. Birds sang, water rippled, the bells on grazing sheep chimed in the distance every time Ralph stopped the car and somewhat frantically took pictures. Was there no end to it? Each time they stopped Carolyn would cry, "Why don't we stop here!" It was a good question, and Ralph explained how the Mormons had faced the same dilemma as they traveled west. Carolyn found the parallel farfetched but agreed she might feel differently about it if she had been raised in the Midwest rather than in the East. Ralph was romantic in a way Carolyn wasn't and took the statements of writers personally, following their suggestions to bolt to Ronda, and what to eat and drink. Of course, she liked that about him, up to a point. Over the winter he had read all the books about Spain and tried to persuade her they should travel with a donkey, Spain being the one place in the world a stranger was safe. If it was so gorgeous, Carolyn asked him, why had his great Mr. Hemingway left it? Ralph thought it had something to do with their civil war. In a gas station on the outskirts of Cordoba the gas attendant had thrown his arms around Ralph, and given him a big hug. He had confused him with some American he had known in the war. It had been difficult for Ralph to persuade him to accept money for the gas. Loyalties of that sort were very touching, and at the same time disturbing. If there had been a war to go to, Ralph would have been tempted to enlist.

This morning the slopes of the mountains were green right up to where the granite shimmered like a sunning lizard. In everything Ralph saw, there was some Hemingway. Admittedly, the bottle of wine he had drunk the most of also helped. Carolyn was more enchanted by the whitewashed villas in the patterned rows of olive trees. But Carolyn was a realist. She knew what they were like inside. While they sat eating lunch, a man with his ox plowed a jagged furrow maybe forty yards long, frequently pausing to glance at the sky, his own shadow, or nothing at all. Waiting for him to reach the end of the row was a strain for Ralph. He was too much of a Peace Corps pilgrim at heart to watch a man kill time like that. If he was going to plow, let him plow and get on with it. One of Ralph's forebears combined spring plowing with memorizing passages from the Bible, which replenished the stories he would tell his family all winter. The Bible he had carried in his pocket was one of Ralph's treasured possessions. Here in this earthly paradise the man seemed lower on the scale than the grazing sheep, with their tinkling bells, or the hog, hobbled in the yard, surrounded by grass plucked that morning.

Carolyn found such dilemmas boring. Couldn't he accept things as they were, and not think so much? The blazing light had brought on one of her headaches, not a little aggravated by the sight of him brooding. She sat in the car while he took more pictures. Even as he did, his pleasure in it was diminished by the knowledge that Carolyn would argue with him about the slides. In her opinion he forgot where he had been, she did not. "To hear Ralph," she would say, "you would think I hadn't been on the trip!" Actually, it was true in a way she would never admit. Those walks Ralph took while Carolyn napped were often the source of his finest shots. "I'm sure he bought that one somewhere," she would say, "I never saw such a place."

These depressing reflections, like Carolyn's headaches, often occurred on those days that "were out of this world," and indicated that they both suffered from too much light. In such euphoric situations they helped Ralph keep his feet on the ground. When he came back to the car, it was surrounded by sheep and Carolyn had run her window up for protection. He could see Carolyn speaking to him, but the bleating of the lambs drowned out what she said. Ralph was disturbed, as he was so often, by the meaning of a scene that seemed to escape him, just as her open mouth spoke words to him that he failed to hear. In this instance she would accuse him of thinking more of his silly pictures than of her safety, using as his excuse this talk about how safe it was in Spain. Carolyn didn't mean these things, she simply found it a relief to talk.

As they climbed toward Ronda, Ralph tried to recall some of the high points of Hemingway's description, but it seemed to be a large impression made up of very few details. That was the art of it. If the gorge he spoke about was a mile deep, it meant the city itself would be a mile high. There was a possibility that Carolyn, who was sensitive to heights, might feel a bit queasy and not want to eat. The actual approach was not at all exciting, but it freshly prepared them for the view from the window of their hotel. Absolutely dazzling: Carolyn stepped back from it with a gasp. Ralph took a roll of shots right there in the room so she would be able to enjoy the view later, safe at home. The altitude left Carolyn bushed, however, and she settled for a nap while Ralph peered around. Three busloads of German tourists—in buses so huge Ralph marveled how they had ever got up there—

crowded the aisles of the small gift shop and gathered in clusters in the patio garden. Many of them, like Carolyn and Ralph, had come to Ronda with a purpose, which was why one saw them huddled in silence before the lifesize statue of Rilke. That in itself surprised Ralph. What had ever brought Rilke to a place like this? He was one of the people Carolyn read and liked so much better than Mr. Hemingway. Rilke would never think of bolting with anybody to such a public spectacle. Ralph's pleasure at the thought of informing Carolyn that her sensitive poet had his statue in the garden was diminished by the fact that he had come here thirteen years before Ralph had been born, and ahead of Hemingway. Ronda was an old tourist mecca, really, and the English and Germans had been coming here for ages. How had Hemingway convinced him he had more or less discovered it?

When the Germans had departed, Ralph had the garden and the view to himself. More than a mile below, lamplight glowed in the windows of the farmhouses. It was like another country, cut off and remote from the one on the rim. Down there it had been dark for an hour or more; here where Ralph stood, the sun flamed on the windows. Ralph took a picture of the one behind which Carolyn slept. It would be hard for her to refute something like that. Several wide brick paths crisscrossed the garden, and one went along the rim, with bays for viewing. In every direction the prospect seemed staggering. In their first years of marriage Ralph had schemed to get Carolyn, somehow, to Arizona, and by stealth, driving at night, up to Bright Angel Lodge on the rim of the Canyon. In the morning she would wake up to face that awesome sight. Her own feeling was that she had come too late for great spectacles. Fellini movies and travel pictures had spoiled it for her. Ralph couldn't seem to understand that actually *being* there, under these circumstances, merely led to a letdown. She would just as soon miss whatever it was as feel something like that.

The path Ralph followed ended so abruptly that he found himself facing a high cable fence, while still preoccupied with his reflections. The two wings of the gate were locked with a chain, but Ralph could see that the path still continued. Weeds grew over it now, and the wall along the rim had breaks here and there that made it dangerous, but in Hemingway's time—not to mention Rilke's—people who came to Ronda did not stop at this fence. They had not come all this way to be fenced in. The tourist walked in those days, he was known as a traveler, and he did not climb from a bus to sit in a bar, or spend a frenzied half hour in the gift shop. He got out and looked around. He wanted his money's worth. Ralph was not so crass, but he had not come to Ronda to peer through a fence. He had not come with that in mind, but as so often happened, that was what he was doing, his fingers hooked in the wires, his eyes at one of the holes. Otherwise he would never have noticed the figure seated on the wall some fifty yards ahead. It was warm there. The sun, in fact, had moved from his lap to his chest and shoulders. He seemed to sit for the portrait that Ralph would like to take. He wore the wide-wale corduroy, with the comfortably loose jacket, the pockets large, the back belted, that Ralph had seen on men he judged to be grounds keepers, guides, watchmen, or whatever. He gave Ralph a nod and a quick smile—free of all "at your service" intimations. Like Ralph, he was a man enjoying the scene. Ralph also thought him so rustically handsome he would like to have a shot of him for Carolyn. Among other things, it would give the scene scale. On second thought it crossed his mind that just such a picture might be available in the hotel lobby. The fellow held a stick, or a cane, in such a manner one knew it was part of his habit, tapping it idly on the hobnailed sole of his boot.

When Ralph remained at the fence, as if expecting to enter,

76

the man rose and came toward him, flicking the weeds with his stick. He greeted Ralph in Spanish, and as if he had been asked, unlocked the chain that closed the gate. He then gestured—in the manner of a man who works with children, or clusters of tourists —for Ralph to come along with him. Concealed beneath the over-growth was a hard stone path that he followed out of long habit, his eyes up ahead. Ralph trailed along behind him, rising slowly to an elevation once cleared but now strewn with boulders from collapsed walls. The view from here—at this hour of the day— looked south along the canyon like the sea's bottom, the upper slopes flaming with a light like the glow from a furnace door. Where had Ralph seen it before? In the inferno paintings of Brueghel and Bosch. At once, that is, indescribable and terrifying. Ralph had no word for it, and apparently none was expected. His companion stood, dyed in the same flaming color, facing what ap-peared to be left the instant following the act of creation, while the earth still cooled. Swallows nestled in the cliffs, and their cries could be heard, changing in pitch as they shifted direction. Their flight on the sky was like fine scratches on film. After a moment of silence the man turned his head and appeared to be surprised that Ralph merely stood there. His eye moved from his face to the camera on his chest.

"No pictures?"

Smilingly, Ralph shrugged. Wasn't it almost impertinent to think that anything but the eye might catch it? The canyon had darkened even as they stood there, as if filling with an inky fluid, rising on the slopes. At the bottom a sinuous road was the exact metallic color of the sky, like the belly of a snake. No, Ralph was not so foolish as to believe he could catch it on film. His com-panion, however, was puzzled.

"No feeelm?" he asked.

Oh, yes, Ralph had film. He nodded to indicate the camera was

loaded; he was just not taking any pictures. This aroused the
man's interest. He tilted his head in the manner of the querulous,
credulous tourist, looking sharply at Ralph. Was he something
new? If he had not come to Ronda for pictures, what then?
Ralph sensed his question clearly enough, but he could do no more
than stand there. His position was not easily explained. He at-
tempted, with some strain, to indicate that he "was taking it all in
with his eyes" rather than his lens. Did it help? The man continued to eye him—a good honest man, Ralph thought, but perhaps a little simple in his thinking. People came here to take pictures. Why didn't Ralph do what was expected of him?

What Ralph *did* do—to distract his gaze, to do something if not
take pictures—was remove from his pocket the bar of chocolate
he had brought all the way from Madrid. Swiss bitter chocolate,
the best; something this sensible fellow would have a taste for.
The piece Ralph offered he accepted, with *muchas gracias*. Chewing up the piece, he was led to comment that he knew Swiss chocolate, and judged it superior. The Swiss made chocolate and
watches. He extended toward Ralph a thick, hairy wrist, orna-
mented with a watch of Swiss manufacture. The one Ralph then
exposed to him received his respectful, somewhat awed, admira-
tion. Such an object with dials and levers he had heard about,
but not seen. It is a commonplace of travel experience that absolute strangers have these congenial moments—not in spite of, but
rather because of, their brevity. With the second piece of chocolate, his friend suggested—this was the feeling of the moment—
that they take seats on the boulders and enjoy the last of the sunset. Knees high, the leveling sun in their eyes, they finished off
the chocolate. Ralph observed how, as his companion peeled off
the foil, he put the wad of wrapping in his pocket. Overhead
were the swallows. Nearer at hand Ralph was conscious of bats.
Fortunately, Carolyn was not present to destroy this moment with

hysterical shrieking, believing, as she did, that bats were no more than horribly flying mice.

Four or five minutes? Ten at the most? Now and then they idly glanced at the display before them, as gods might be amused by the northern lights. On the cliffs the remarkable tints seemed to bleed and dry like watercolors. His friend was the first to rise —not without a groan—and extend toward Ralph a helping hand. Why should something so common be so memorable? In his brusque matter-of-factness Ralph sensed that he too felt it. He was not so simple he did not know that this moment was something special. They walked back toward the hotel, the man ahead, Ralph trailing, turning once for a last glance at what vanished as they were looking. In that instant, it seemed, the air turned cold. They continued to the gate, where Ralph, in an involuntary gesture, turned and placed his left hand on the man's shoulder, and offered him his right. His companion lowered his eyes as if to locate Ralph's hand in the darkness. Yes, he actually looked. It seemed so droll a thing to do—something you might expect from a natural comic—that Ralph actually smiled. He also reached for the hand that was partially offered, gripped it firmly, then said *Vaya con Dios*—only one of many things he would soon enough regret. The man muttered something, but Ralph was so moved by his own feelings, his own generous impulses, he heard nothing but the wind of his own emotion.

Fortunately, the gate had been opened, and he was able to turn and make his escape. *Make his escape?* Was that the first suspicion that he had misread the situation? He did not look back. The fresh smarting of his face, a warmness all over his body, was not the result of his downhill walking. No, he was blushing. He was overheated with embarrassment. So clear to him now he could only go along with his head down, thankful for the darkness, was that this man had looked to his hand for something

Ralph had not offered. A payment for services rendered.

Least of all the things in this world he had expected, or wanted, was a handshake. A *handshake!* He must be standing there, shaking with laughter. This Americano who offered him a handshake. Was it believable? He would now go home with empty pockets but a story, a tale, that would last forever, be repeated by his children, conceivably become a legend of sorts at Ronda. The big Americano tourist who had gripped his hand, and urged him to go with God.

From a niche behind the statue of Rilke Ralph paused long enough for a quick glance rearward. Had he gone? No, he was still there, but the rising tide of darkness had submerged him. He was all of one color, at this distance, his face the weathered tan of his corduroy, but Ralph had the distinct impression that his teeth were exposed in a smile. That could have been wrong. Maybe he merely stood there stupefied. Ralph might have walked, unseen, into the lobby, where the lights were now on, a fire was burning, and the woman who stood before it, warming her backside, wore a miniskirt. Was it something he could speak about to Carolyn? How would it be phrased? Would she understand his failure to grasp he was in another country? And if not, where he was, *how things were?* This man had done him a service—could it have been more obvious? He had opened a gate and given him a short tour—and on the return Ralph had offered him his hand. Would it be sensible, would it be believable, that Ralph considered him an equal, such a fleeting but true friend, really, that to have offered him money would have falsified their brief meeting, and reduced something gold to something brass? Carolyn would only make one of those gargle sounds in her throat. The other thing was—a sudden chill brought it home—that what he had been thinking of all the time was the high value of his own sensations, and in this intoxication he felt these sensations would be shared with his companion. As Ralph valued him, surely he would be moved to value Ralph, a fumbling but generous tourist who in a kind of Eucharist offered him chocolate. In this brief wordless drama two illusions had suffered, but was there any doubt whose illusion had been the greater? Both stories were good, but Ralph's would be one he kept to himself.

*Printed July 1973 in Santa Barbara*
*for the Black Sparrow Press by Noel Young.*
*Design by Barbara Martin. This edition is*
*published in paper wrappers; there are*
*500 hardcover copies; & 226 copies have*
*been handbound in boards by Earle Gray*
*& are numbered & signed by the author.*